# THIS BOOK IS BROUGHT TO YOU BY

# THE MAGNUS MAXIMUS 10X

### PROFESSIONAL-GRADE MAGNIFYING GLASS

## THE PREFERRED CHOICE OF MASTER DETECTIVES!

Beveled glass, hand carved in the mountains of Bavaria, Idaho!

Objects look ten times bigger and twenty times more disgusting!

Comfortable rubber handle. Great grip for serves and backhands!

Handy hidden soup spoon for the hungry detective!

I just discovered a secret treasure map that, for some reason, just burst into flames!

I just used it to track strange critter footprints on the school playground!

GRRRRR!

FROM GET A CLUE

# KIRK SCROGGS

# SNOOP TROOP

## IT CAME FROM BENEATH THE PLAYGROUND

SCHOLASTIC INC.

No part of this publication may be reproduced, stored in a retrieval system, or transmitted in any form or by any means, electronic, mechanical, photocopying, recording, or otherwise, without written permission of the publisher. For information regarding permission, write to Little, Brown Books for Young Readers, a division of Hachette Book Group, Inc., 237 Park Avenue, 15th Floor, New York, NY 10017.

ISBN 978-0-545-83022-5

Published by Scholastic Inc., 557 Broadway, New York, NY 10012, by arrangement with Little, Brown Books for Young Readers, a division of Hachette Book Group, Inc. SCHOLASTIC and associated logos are trademarks and/or registered trademarks of Scholastic Inc.

12 11 10 9 8 7 6 5 4 3 2 1                    15 16 17 18 19 20/0

Printed in the U.S.A.                    40

First Scholastic printing, January 2015

*To Isaac*

*Special thanks to
Steve Deline; Joanna Stampfel-Volpe;
Diane, Corey, Candace, and Charlotte Scroggs;
Camilla and Marisa Deline; Joe Kocian;
Mark Mayes; and a twenty-one-Snoop-Troop
salute to Andrea Spooner, Deirdre Jones,
Tracy Shaw, and the whole Little, Brown crew.
Woo-hoo!*

# An Important Message
# from the Narrator

# Yo! Attention, all you wannabe detectives out there!

Justice needs your help. Some lowlife, sneaker-sniffin' criminal is stealing all the fun from the kids of Murkee Elementary School. Help my detectives put this creep behind bars. Examine each page of this case file closely for clues, especially if you see a magnifying glass like the one below. I'd help out, but I'm too busy looking for Rocco the Racketeering Raccoon. Now, where could that little fleabag be?

Find Rocco!

# CHAPTER 1

## BY THE BOOK

**A**fter school at Murkee Elementary...

Silence creeps over the halls like a spilled Blue Raspberry Icee....

Chalk dust settles on the cold classroom floors like volcanic ash....

Tumbleweeds roll through the empty playground, tumbling over and over, like a narrator who just won't shut up....

**The day is Wednesday.**
**The time is 4:25 PM.**
**Remember that!**
**All that we hold dear**
**could depend on it!**

That's fourth-grader Logan Lang sitting in the dark, dank library, just like she does every day after school, surrounded by her friends....

And when I say "friends," I mean mystery books,

crime novels,

and twisted tales of suspense....

They're all she has in this cold, lonely world.

Okay, I think they get it. I'm a little *too* into mystery books.

# A BRIEF HISTORY OF LOGAN

This is her idea of being less nerdy.

Miss Perusa, the librarian, gives Logan just five more minutes to grab as many small, furry animal mystery books as she can find.

But before Logan can check out her giant stack
of books, a voice blares out across the library!

It's coming from her combination police radio/
lunch box....

It picks up a hundred
frequencies and
smells like bologna
and corn chips.

Logan tries to gingerly tiptoe down the hall toward the exit when...

# It's Gustavo Muchomacho, Logan's arch-nuisance!

He's conducting his weekly after-school Macho Cop Club for Kids meeting.

# AN EVEN BRIEFER HISTORY
# OF GUSTAVO

### AGE: 1 YEAR

### AGE: 10 YEARS

# CHAPTER 2
## MERRY-GONE-MISSING

**H**urling Rivers Amusement Park...

When Logan arrives, the place is taped off like an unopened birthday present and crawling with cops.

CRIME SCENE
ING!* WARNING!* WAR
LICE AT WORK        POLICE AT
ENTER * DO NOT OPEN UNTIL CHRIST

That's Captain Mosely of the Murkee City Police
Department....

Boys, this one's a doozy.
I've heard of stolen cars,
stolen paintings, stolen glances
across a crowded room...
but a stolen merry-go-round?
That's a new one on me!

Sure enough, there's just a big hole in the ground where the carousel used to be.

23

I don't think you're supposed to go past that police tape.

Good point. Carry on.

What have you got there?

I didn't know you could draw.

That was nice of you.

While the cops eat the evidence, Logan sets out in search of her own clues. Somewhere on the deserted boardwalk, she gets the creepy sensation that someone is hiding nearby.

# Suddenly,
## a sniffly old man bursts out of a pile of stuffed animals!

It's Izzy Hurling, owner of Hurling Rivers Amusement Park, and he's quite sneezy.

29

# DRAW THE SUSPECT!

**Listen to Old Man Hurling's description and draw the culprit on a piece of scratch paper, the chalkboard, or your mom's favorite tablecloth!**

They were really short and pudgy with brown, spiky hair all over. They had itty-bitty beady eyes. Their snouts were pointy. Their arms and legs were stubby. They had long claws that were covered in dirt.

33

All of a sudden, a pint-size detective with two tons of attitude and a one-ton mustache is on the scene....

Something about this guy looks familiar. Logan can't quite place him, but she already has the urge to smack him with an overcooked bratwurst.

**It's not Officer Chuck Brawn at all! It's Gustavo Muchomacho in a cheap fake mustache!**

39

Ahem! Hey, you two, maybe you should team up like Captain Mosely suggested. Logan, with your smarts and Gustavo's...uh...enthusiasm, you could cause twice as much damage.

Where's that strange voice coming from?

Oh, that's just the narrator. He's pretty sassy.

Well, how about it? Team Logan and Gustavo.

As Gustavo takes off, Logan is left all alone....

Before she heads home, a chill nips at her neck and a strange feeling comes over her—like an evil presence is still lurking close by.

This just in: An amusement park merry-go-round has gone missing! Cops say it was taken by moles or maybe just some punks who wanted to take it out for a spin!
BREAKING NEWS
MISSING!
THE LOCO LOCAL
50¢
MERRY-GO-ROUND STOLEN!
MOLES MAY BE TO BLAME
HAVE YOU SEEN THIS RIDE?
COPS DESCRIBE CAROUSEL AS WHITE WITH RED STRIPES, FIFTY HORSEPOWER, OFTEN ACCOMPANIED BY ORGAN MUSIC
NATIONAL FABRICATOR
MOLES
MAKE OFF WITH MERRY-GO-ROUND!
BOTTOMLESS PIT
IN OTHER NEWS, HURLIN PARK INTRODUCES NEW ATTRACTION, THE BOTTOMLESS PIT!

# CHAPTER 3
## THAT SINKING FEELING

The next morning, Logan arrives at school tired and cranky from staying up all night watching the news reports about the theft. The smell of trouble hangs like bad air freshener in a gas station bathroom. Everywhere she looks, she thinks she sees moles. Principal Shrub tries to keep nervous students calm.

Inside, the school is abuzz with stories of more mole mayhem. It seems the merry-go-round isn't the only thing missing in action.

Farther down the hall, Logan stumbles upon something even more disturbing....

Before Logan can do anything rash, the school suddenly starts to shake and

Logan and Gustavo run outside to find the playground swings swinging out of control and the seesaws teetering and tottering violently. Everything seems to be sinking into the earth!

Not one to stand by and watch all her fellow students get pulled under, Logan swings out onto the monkey bars to rescue little Charlie Richards!

Gustavo jumps onto one end of the seesaw to save Bobby Bing, but for some reason, Bobby goes sailing into the air without even saying good-bye.

Wait! Don't go. I'm trying to rescue you!

Then Logan fishes Holly Peterson out of the sandbox with a tetherball pole while Gustavo directs the rest of the kids down the slide to safety.

When the dust finally settles, all that's left of the playground is a giant hole.

While Principal Shrub is pelted with sand, Logan and Gustavo peer over into the dark, foreboding pit.

# CHAPTER 4
## BEG, BURROW, OR STEAL

**L**ogan and Gustavo explore the creepy cave beneath the playground. It's dark, moist, and chilly, like a congested polar bear's nostril. And did I mention it's dark? I mean really dark.

Gustavo's Illumistache quickly reveals a huge pile of boulders blocking their path.

A high-pitched, chipmunky voice blares out of a deranged mole's walkie-talkie....

If the students of Murkee Elementary want to see their merry-go-round, toys, and playground again, they will leave their lunch money on the second base of the softball field by 3:33 PM!

Perhaps if we could speak to you without your army of moles, we could negotiate....

If these critters want to negotiate, they'll have to do it with my foot! Prepare for combat!

The moles attack Gustavo with a Mighty Mach 5 Mega Maneuver, which he blocks with a Shaolin Super Shield!

Then they hit Logan with a Hyper Hedgehog High Kick, but she avoids it using her Timid Tenderfoot Technique!

It's the greatest martial arts fight scene ever! Unfortunately, since it's pitch-black, no one can see it. At least we saved some serious money on illustrations.

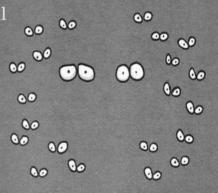

Logan and Gustavo finally crawl back out of the hole, beaten and exhausted.

That blubbering glob of beef jerky is Ignas Scurge, the school bully....

# CHAPTER 5

## CURVEBALL

**M**urkee Elementary softball field, 3:30 PM. The lunch money is waiting on second base. Something else is waiting, too—ten hidden kids ready to pounce on whoever shows up to nab it.

DRINK

SWIG

TRY CHERRY, GRAPE, OR WILD ONION!

YOU CAN DO IT... PROBABLY!

Spot the hidden kids!

You two look pretty prepared.

That's a pretty big Tylenol.

So, Logan and Gustavo wait...

and wait...

and wait...

It's 3:33 PM. I guess they're not coming.

71

# Suddenly, a mole on a hang glider swoops in from above and swipes the bag of dough!

I've changed my mind! I want all of your lunch money for the next three weeks dropped off at Hurling Rivers tomorrow at 5:27 PM. Then maybe you'll get your stuff back! If you don't comply, I will strike again....
This case is gonna call for a little after-school detection.
Criminals these days! You just can't take their word on anything!

# CHAPTER 6
## HOMEWORK

**W**hen the last bell rings, Logan reluctantly lets Gustavo come over to work on the case.

If you're wondering why Logan's office is in an ice-cream truck, well, Logan's mom is an ice-cream man, uh, I mean *person*. She just got a fancy new truck with GPS and automatic fro-yo dispensers, so she's letting Logan use her old one to set up shop.

Gustavo is amazed
by Logan's collection
of mystery books...

her library of detective
shows on video...

and her trophy from
the Murkee City Break
Dancing and Beat Box
Championship?

Whoa! Look at those
fly dance pants!

Give me those!
I was, uh, in
disguise on
an important
undercover
operation.

Wheelie's 114 in dog years and has wheels on his hindquarters to help him get around. Most folks think he's always angry, but he actually has many moods:

Grumpy

Cranky

Furious

Cheesed off

Disappointed

About to bite you

Now that Gustavo and Wheelie are acquainted, Logan pulls out a marker and doodles on the world's biggest whiteboard.

What we know so far:

Takes things kids like

Has high-pitched voice

She jots down everything that they know about
the suspect.

Gustavo offers his expertise as well....

Hey! Isn't he the guy who wrote the nerdy mole book you got from the library?

Logan whips out a map of the city to look for
Dr. Yonder's office at the Bureau of Burrowing.

# CHAPTER 7
## DEEPLY DISTURBING

Twenty minutes later, Logan and Gustavo roll up on their skateboards to the Bureau of Burrowing, in the heart of the Five Boroughs, in between Budrow's Burnished Bedroom Sets and Bureaus and Dos Burros Burritos. The joint is quiet. Too quiet. It's got Gustavo spooked.

Don't worry. Wheelie's here to protect us.

But who's gonna protect me from Wheelie?

Before entering the building, Logan reminds Gustavo and Wheelie that Dr. Yonder might help them solve the case, but he could also be the culprit. In fact...

## everyone they talk to is a suspect! Remember that! The fate of humanity could depend on it!

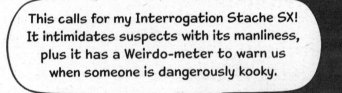

This calls for my Interrogation Stache SX! It intimidates suspects with its manliness, plus it has a Weirdo-meter to warn us when someone is dangerously kooky.

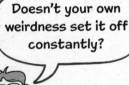

Doesn't your own weirdness set it off constantly?

Once they're inside, a hole in the floor opens, and a doctor bearing a big bowl of candy rises up. He offers the confections to Logan and Gustavo.

I suppose you're here about the curious criminal-mole incidents. It's certainly the most exciting development in burrowing mammals since the synchronized swimming shrews of Sri Lanka!

Don't mind if I do, Doc!

WHISTLER'S MOLE

Logan decides to put the pressure on Dr. Yonder....

91

Dr. Yonder gives the kids the grand tour of the underworld where he studies all things that live underground.

Dr. Yonder's lab is chock-full of beakers and gizmos and mole specimens. Across the room, Logan spots a strange device that resembles a bullhorn crossed with a fire extinguisher.

Dr. Yonder escorts them to his swanky office. Logan stops beating around the bush and asks him where he was yesterday at 4:25 PM, the time the merry-go-round went bye-bye.

96

Logan and Gustavo take off through Dr. Yonder's hall of prehistoric mole bones, with Wheelie burning rubber in the rear.

# They reach the exit only to discover Dr. Yonder brandishing a long metal torture device!

Back at Logan's ice-cream truck headquarters, our two detectives discuss the case over a couple of cold Fudgysickles.

**Whew! What a day! That guy was a total loony bird. I say we turn him in to Cap'n Mosely pronto!**

**Not so fast! Just because someone thinks a preserved, hairy critter is his mom doesn't make him a criminal. We need hard evidence!**

CHOCO-BURRITO

FUDGY SICKLE
IT'S WHUT'S FOR DINNER

I hate to interrupt your all-you-can-eat Fudgysickle buffet, but Izzy Hurling is being interviewed on the local news!

# CHAPTER 8

## IZZY GUILTY?

**H**urling Rivers Amusement Park. It's nearing closing time, and the park is as quiet as a mouse with a sock in its mouth. It's the perfect opportunity for Logan to get some answers.

They find Izzy in his office. He looks frantic and nervous as he flips through stacks of bills on his desk.

105

Izzy's violent allergic reaction to Wheelie leaves Logan and Gustavo with no choice but to leave his office empty-handed. They had thought this visit would bring answers, but instead, they leave with more questions and covered in old-man sneeze particles.

Wheelie takes it particularly hard. Just look at that sad face.

Our discouraged detectives slowly make their way out of the park and...Hey! Where are you two headed off to so fast?

Well, perhaps I should take this moment to remind you that the next lunch-money drop-off is

# tomorrow at 5:27 PM!!!

No pressure. No pressure at all.

# CHAPTER 9
## DETENTION MOUNTS

The next morning at school, Principal Shrub is collecting lunch money from all the students, and, like a masseuse wearing boxing gloves, it rubs Logan the wrong way.

Seems like Principal Shrub is awfully eager to take our lunch money. I think he might be another suspect.

Hmmm...he is a pro at sucking the fun out of life. Maybe he's turned it into a lucrative venture.

MUSTACHES OF ANCIENT ROME

ANT FARM

SNACK CAKES

HISTORY

The sound of music suddenly catches their attention. It's the school bully, Ignas Scurge, and he's at his locker whistling a happy tune.

The sight of Ignas Scurge smiling and being nice sends Gustavo into a tizzy. Clearly, the case is breaking him.

It's all too much to handle! Missing merry-go-rounds, hang gliding moles, Ignas being nice! The world's gone nuts!

Don't let the pressure get to you, rookie. We just need to look at all the evidence one last time. The answer is there!

SUSPECT

So, during lunch, instead of pouring gravy over Salisbury steak like the other students, Logan and Gustavo pore over the clues, notes, and doodles from the case....

Finally, Logan plants her finger on one of her doodles!

## An Important Message from the Narrator

Hiya, punks! Since you wanna be detectives so bad, I thought I'd give you a chance to figure out whodunit before Logan and Gustavo spoil it in the next chapter. If you're stumped, go back and look at each page with a magnifying glass labeled "Suspect" or "Clue," like the ones right here.

Look closely!

SUSPECT

Read carefully!

CLUE

# Which one of these suspects is a low-down dirty crook?

 **IZZY HURLING?** He sure needed the money.

 **DR. DEEP YONDER?** He's a weirdo who knows his moles.

 **IGNAS SCURGE?** He loves stealing lunch money.

 **PRINCIPAL SHRUB?** He was all about paying off the thief.

## Turn the page to find who dood it!

# CHAPTER 10
## A REVEALING ADDRESS

**H**urling Rivers Amusement Park, 5:25 PM. Logan and Gustavo have three weeks' worth of lunch money waiting for the thief. But, to make things more interesting, they've also invited the entire student body of Murkee Elementary, the city police force, the media, and a dog on wheels.

Gustavo steps up to a podium in front of the spectators and law enforcement officials. He's wearing his Studly Stache LX to impress the crowd.

Ladies and gentlemen! One of you is a filthy, rotten criminal! The rest of you, I'm sure, are lovely people. We have called you here to reveal the identity of the scoundrel who has been training moles to steal the fun away from our city's youth.

WELCOME CITIZENS

NO FLASH PHOTOGRAPHY

JUSTICE

120

Logan turns her attention to the owner of Hurling Rivers....

Izzy Hurling could have staged the theft of his merry-go-round to get the ransom money. His amusement park is in dire financial trouble.

Lucky for him, though, he's allergic to animal fur. There's no way he could have worked with moles without having a disgusting allergic reaction!

IZZY HURLING

AMUSEMENT PARK

UNPAID BILLS

BILLS
+ #
# #

NOSE SPRAY + = AAAA... CHOOO!

Even the school principal isn't above suspicion.

The crowd roars with laughter. Principal Shrub
doesn't take it too well.

With Shrub ruled out as the criminal, it leaves just one other suspect....

Uh, call me crazy, but I think you need proof before you can just make accusations like that.

Suddenly, Ignas jumps up onto the podium like a frog with ants in his button-fly jeans and confesses to the whole kit and caboodle.

All right! I did it! Those moles helped me collect a hundred times more lunch money than my usual shtick! You guys even thought I had gone all nice. Suckers!

I should have known a bully never changes his ways. Just like a tiger never changes his stripes and a fourth-grade boy never changes his underwear!

Amen to that, sister!

SO WHUT?

JUSTICE

Captain Mosely steps up to make the arrest.

With a mighty tremor, the earth suddenly opens up like an overstuffed piñata. Hundreds of attack moles leap out and wreak havoc on the public. But that's just a warm-up....

Right behind the normal-size moles is one abnormal, gargantuan, *gigante*, behemoth-tastic robo-mole, built from the missing merry-go-round and scrap metal from the stolen playground!

# The mecha-beast lays waste to the park!

The cries of stranded park riders grab Logan's attention, and she swings out like Tarzan to rescue a tot off the Junior Jungle Terror Cruise!

Wheelie rolls out onto the bumper-car course to save a terrified mother and her swaddled babe!

And Gustavo rescues the last funnel cake from a bubbling pit of hot grease!

Come to Papa!

Dr. Deep Yonder steps in to offer his expertise. If Logan and Gustavo can activate his Mole Disser 5000, tragedy can be averted.

Unfortunately, the device got lost in the stampede!
Whatever shall we do? Oh me, oh my!

Logan takes matters into her own hands. And when I say "matters," I mean Gustavo's 'stache.

With a mighty toss, Logan lets the facial hair fly!

The Mole Disser 5000 unleashes a stream of insults!

Even the metal monster collapses in a twisted heap! It must have been sensitive to insults as well.

But Captain Mosely has other ideas....

139

# CHAPTER 11
## MAKE THAT A DOUBLE SCOOP

**1411** Baskerville Lane, 4:34 PM. A bold new detective duo sits in their refurbished office, ready for cases of mystery, intrigue, and mild excitement to come pouring in.

To make time for the new business, Gustavo has to give up his weekly Macho Cop Club for Kids meetings.

They come up with a clever name using the process of elimination—meaning Logan quickly eliminates all of Gustavo's suggestions.

They hire a friendly canine bodyguard.

And Logan hooks Gustavo up with his own desk, filled with six-month-old Fudgysickles.

Then they sit and wait...and wait...

and wait…and wait….

# DOODLE SNOOPS

## CLASSIFIED

**Warning:
The following secret files
may require doodling,
scribbling, heavy thinking,
and possible yodeling!**

Hey! If you don't own this book,
make sure you only doodle on a piece
of scrap paper. If Miss Perusa finds
any drawing on school property,
she might staple your big toe
to a math book!

MYSTERY
FICTION
HISTORY

LIBRARIAN

# HOW TO DRAW

**1.** Start with the eyes, like the lenses from a pair of sunglasses.

**2.** Just like school, they need pupils.

**3.** Add a cute little nose.

**4.** Then the face, like a soup bowl with ears.

**5.** Then some hair, like your mom's drapes.

**6.** Finish with some shoulders and a sly grin. There you have it!

# HOW TO DRAW GUSTAVO

**1.** Start with two orbs, like two plump olives.

**2.** Draw a schnoz, like a fat jelly bean.

**3.** Add a head, like a large soda with ears.

**4.** Don't forget the stylish hair.

**5.** How about a manly mustache?

**6.** Hire your three-year-old brother to color it in and voilà!

# HOW TO DRAW

## AN ANGRY MOLE

**1.** Draw a snout, like a balloon with two strings.

**2.** Add some angry eyes.

**3.** How about some jagged teeth?

**4.** And an arm with sharp claws, like a pointy garden tool.

**5.** Give it a terrible case of back hair.

**6.** And don't forget the pretty bow! Congrats! You're done!

# HOW TO DRAW
## WHEELIE

**1.** Start with two mad eyeballs.

**2.** Add a snout, like an upside-down turnip.

**3.** Give him a shaggy mustache, like two bird wings.

**4.** Some snarly teeth and a beard.

**5.** Add floppy ears, like a bunny with a fur condition. And a long neck, too.

**6.** Be sure to add plenty of slobber for authenticity. Now, back off! He just might bite you!

151

# WHAT'S UNDER LOGAN'S MAGNIFYING GLASS?

## Sketch the magnified clue!

- It has six legs.
- It oozes slime.
- It has three eyes.
- It wears high-top sneakers.
- It sings karaoke!

**What's in Wheelie's dog bowl and why does it smell like blue cheese?**

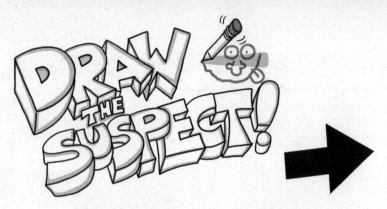

## Something's eating Miss Myrtle's potted plants up on the fifth floor! Help the Snoop Troop catch the culprit by sketching the suspect. Here's an eyewitness description:

- It's tall with four long, skinny legs.
- It has splotchy spots all over.
- It has a seven-foot-long neck!
- It has a tail with a tuft of hair on the end.
- It has big eyes with luscious lashes.
- It was last seen with a mouthful of chewed petunias.

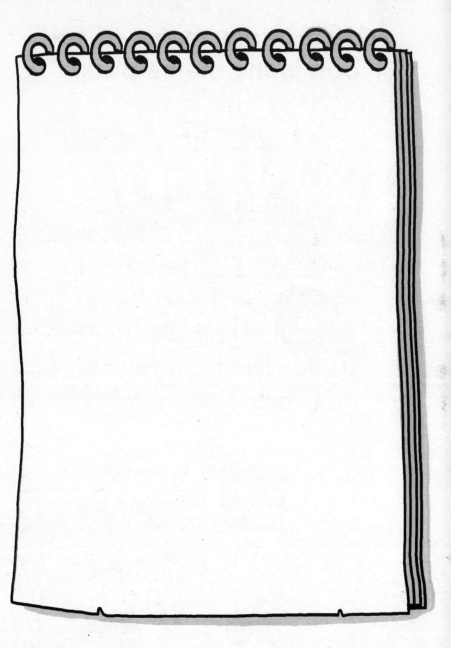

# Hide as many moles as you can in the theme park!

# Make sure they're extra hidden! The Snoop Troop is here to sniff them out!

Fill in all the gross details!

# WORD SEARCH

```
A B M B L N X Z D F U R R Y A C D
Q I D P E T S T O R E U P W I S L
U T N O L H L C I D K R A N S O M
I E S O B U N D E R G R O U N D J
P R A I R I E D O G Y F K D B Q H
S R T H N C C E U L O R F M C L A
T U R R Y L L A B O R A T O R Y I
E B A Q D U Y D P I P U R L F E R
A T U N N E L I K G A D J E T S Y
L B Z R O S W G P B U R R O W E S
```

## FIND THE WORDS INVOLVING CRIMINAL UNDERGROUND CRITTERS!

Answers on page 168!

**Answers on page 168!**

FLYING POLKA-DOT ELEPHANT MOLE

JUGGLING TWO-HEADED ROBO-MOLE

SABER-TOOTHED, BREAK-DANCING, AQUA MOLE

# DOODLE SNOOPS ANSWER KEY

## WORD SEARCH:

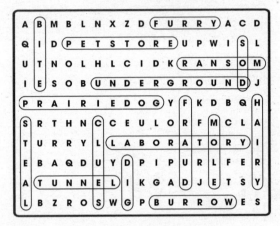

## MOLE DISSER 5000 PARTS:

1. Page 164: on the clown's hat
2. Page 164: in the man's hand
3. Page 165: on the counter by the condiments
4. Page 165: the lady's earring
5. Page 165: on the boy's head
6. Page 165: on the ground under the bench

# KIRK SCROGGS

is the author and illustrator of the Tales of a Sixth-Grade Muppet series and the Wiley & Grampa's Creature Features series. He lives in Los Angeles.